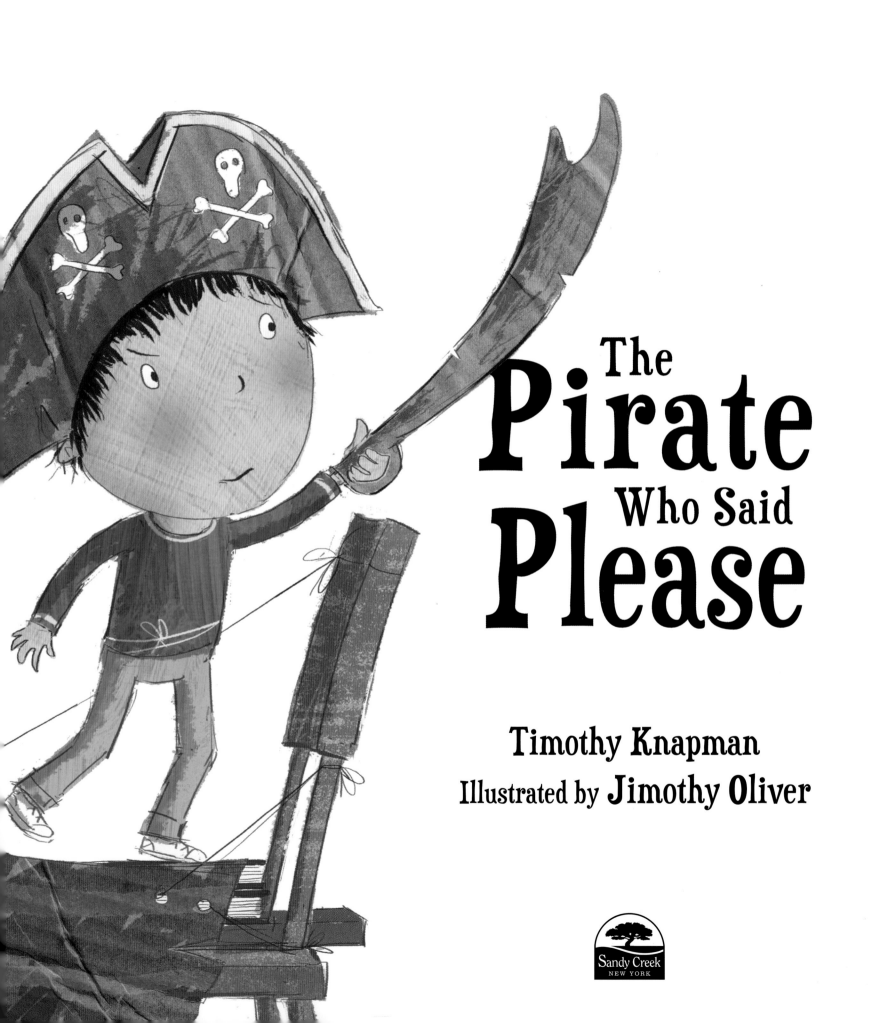

The Pirate Who Said Please

Timothy Knapman

Illustrated by **Jimothy Oliver**

Sandy Creek
NEW YORK

Pirate Jim is a **pirate king** who rules the seven seas.

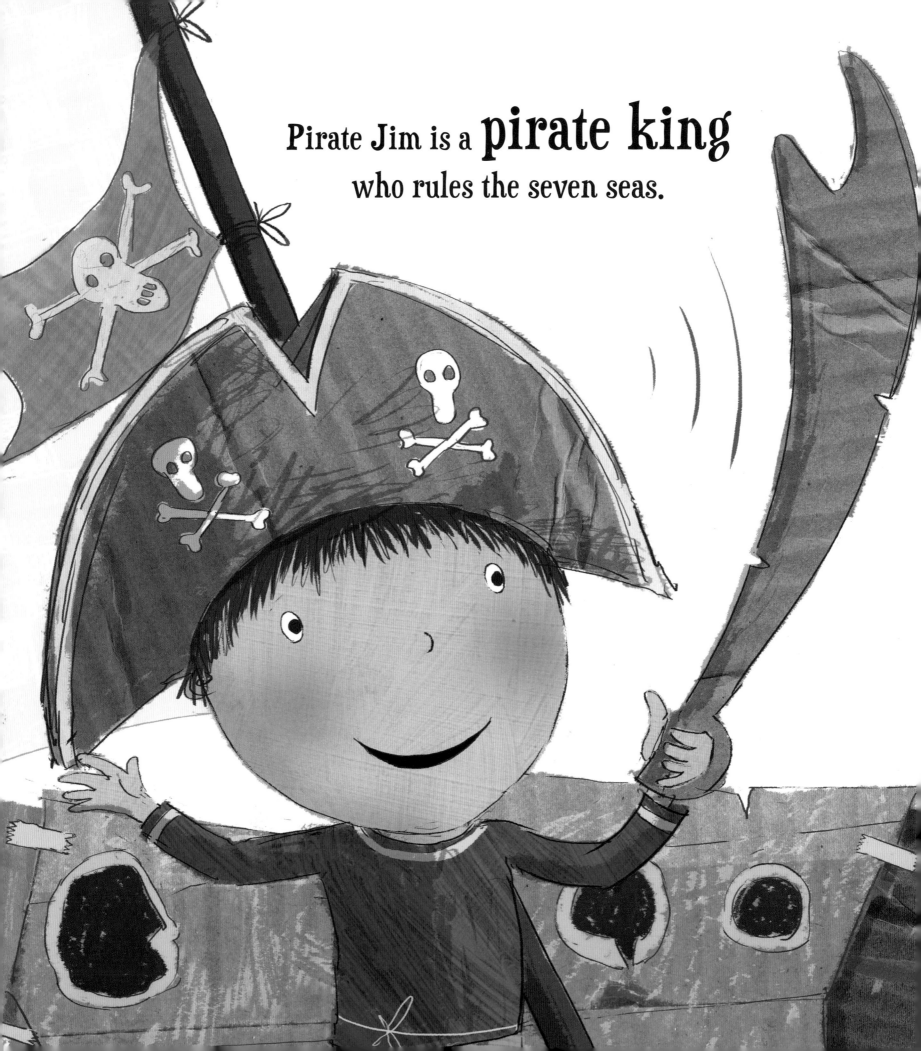

But Jim is very **well behaved**
and never forgets to say
please.

Just one look at his cardboard sword
and all the sharks **shiver** and **shake**.

But he always says,
"Thank you, Grandma!"
when she gives him cookies or cake.

His **pirate ship** is a scary sight,
the terror of the living room!

But he remembered to say, "Hey, Mom,
please may I borrow the chair and broom?"

Pirate Jim **loves** a pirate feast—
it's his favorite **pirate treat!**

But he never forgets to ask **nicely**
if he wants some more to eat.

He captures lots of **treasure chests**
without a fuss or a fight.
You see, people give him lots of things...

...because he's so **polite**.

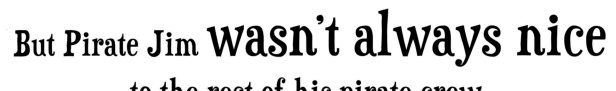

But Pirate Jim **wasn't always nice**
to the rest of his pirate crew.

He was **rude** and **mean** and hosed them down
until they were all soaked through.

He **snatched** whichever toys they brought
before the games had begun.

So the next time they **didn't bring any**,
and the games weren't all that much fun.

At parties he'd forever be shouting,
"Give me more pirate food!"

So people stopped inviting him over
and thought this little pirate **rude**.

When he told his crew what to do,
he **wouldn't** say "**please**" - he'd **moan!**

So they left him behind on an island –
faraway and all **alone**.

And that's how **Pirate Jim** was taught
the most important lesson you'll learn:
be **polite** to other people,
and they'll be polite in **return**.

So take note, you salty dogs,
of the tale of **Pirate Jim**.
If you want to be a pirate king,
then you must **behave** like him.

Always say, "**please**" when you're asking
and always **remember to thank**.
Or you'll make the pirates angry,
and you'll have to walk the **plank!**

An Imprint of Sterling Publishing Co., Inc.
1166 Avenue of the Americas
New York, NY 10036

Text © 2012 by QEB Publishing, Inc.
Illustrations © 2012 by QEB Publishing, Inc.

ISBN 978-1-4351-5601-2

Manufactured in Guangdong, China
Lot #:
6 8 10 9 7
10/17

Editor: Alexandra Koken
Designer: Andrew Crowson
Consultant: Cecilia A. Essau